For Jaymes, who brightens every day. ~ R. C.

With heartfelt thanks to Dr. Feuillet and his family. ~ V. D.

Lunette, The True Story of the Tooth Fairy

Written by Robin Cruise ~ Illustrated by Valeria Docampo

In a time long ago, there was no Tooth Fairy.

NO TOOTH FAIRY? It seems impossible, and yet it is true. Those many years ago, when children like you lost a tooth, they didn't tuck it beneath a pillow. And they didn't wake up the next morning to discover that the Tooth Fairy had left a small gift for them. But all that changed when a kind fairy made a human friend. This is their true story ...

IT WAS MIDSUMMER'S EVE. The fairies had gathered at dusk in Moonglow Glen just as they did every year, to celebrate the sunny days ahead.

This was Lunette's favorite day. But she sighed as she looked up from the small star-shaped pillow she was embroidering. "Oh, Little Mouse," she said. "Flynn turns secret ingredients into magic dust. And Blossom helps the flowers bloom ... Every one of the fairy folk has a special talent, except for me."

Little Mouse gazed up at his friend. Lunette was good at needlework, collecting coins and shiny baubles, and making friends. But none of those things seemed special enough to her.

The next morning, the Fairy Queen met Lunette in the garden. "It is Midsummer's Day," the queen said. "And yet you aren't joyful. Why is that, Lunette?"

"Another year has passed, and I still don't know what my special talent is," Lunette said sadly.

"Ah," said the queen. "You must figure that out for yourself, Lunette. What special talent do *you* want to make your own?"

"I wish I could be brave and clever," Lunette said. "And *kind*—especially to all who are afraid."

"I see," said the queen. She reached for a quill and paper, and then she wrote: *Brave. Clever. Kind.* Handing the paper to Lunette, she said, "Carry this with you always."

"Good queen, is it *enough* to be brave, clever, and kind?" Lunette whispered.

A smile brightened the queen's face. "We'll have to see, won't we?"

That afternoon, Lunette and Little Mouse stretched in the sunshine together.

"I've often wondered why this valley is called *Moonglow Glen*," Lunette said. "Even when the moon is full at night, it is dark here. If I were truly clever, I would fill the sky with stars to make the glen as bright at night as it is by day."

The sound of loud cries nearby startled Lunette and Little Mouse. "That's Blossom!" Lunette said.

"And it sounds like Flynn, too!" said Little Mouse. They scampered off to find them.

Lunette and Little Mouse joined their friends, who were hiding behind a tree stump. Blossom clasped one hand over her mouth and pointed with the other.

"It's a human child!" Flynn gasped. "And he is *crying*."

It wasn't every day that the fairies happened upon a human child. Lunette peered at the boy, while Flynn and Blossom backed away timidly.

"Why is he sad?" Lunette wondered aloud. Her own heart ached a little, and she flew over without hesitating for even a moment.

"Hello," she whispered.

The boy turned wide-eyed toward the quiet voice. "Oh, hello. I'm Lucas."
He blinked hard several times. "You are so small! Am I dreaming?"

"Definitely *not*!" Lunette said. "I am one of the fairy folk. Most people can't
even *see* us. You must be ... *special*. Why are you crying? Maybe I can help."

"I don't think s-s-so," he sputtered. "My tooth is loose. I know it's going
to fall out so a big one can grow in—but I'm scared."

"I understand," Lunette replied. "Even *thinking* about my teeth falling
out makes me scared, too."

Lunette had an idea. "When your tooth falls out, let a light shine in your bedroom that night," she said. "If you hide your tooth as a gift for me, I'll use it to make something magical."

She paused, then added, "There's one more thing you must know. My name is Lunette, but please don't call me that. We fairy folk don't use our names with humans. It's part of our magic."

Waving good-bye, Lunette hurried away. She thought of the stars she loved, shimmering above Moonglow Glen, and her heart raced. She was eager to turn her idea into magic.

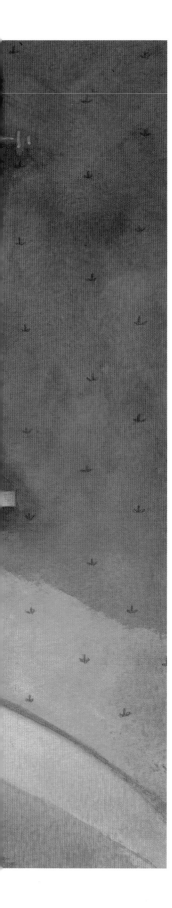

Lucas's tooth fell out that very evening while
he was slurping pudding with his granddad.
It barely hurt at all.

Granddad flashed Lucas a smile and wrapped the
tooth in his handkerchief so it wouldn't get lost.

They both laughed when Lucas poked his tongue
through the gap where his tooth had been.

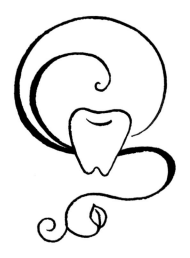

Lucas's granddad tucked him in snugly. "Shall we let your light shine while you sleep?" he asked.

Lunette had said to let a light shine! "Granddad," Lucas whispered, "can you help me hide my tooth? It's a gift for ... a small friend. And I want to write her a note, too."

"We'll hide it under your pillow, Lucas," Granddad said. "And I have another idea." He left for a few moments, and returned with a quill, some paper, and a honey cake. "Everyone likes sweets!"

Lucas wrote a note to Lunette and tucked it under the honey cake.

That night, Lunette noticed a light shining from across the glen. "Little Mouse!" she called. "That's Lucas's house—we must hurry." She grabbed a shiny coin and slipped it into the pocket of the star-shaped pillow she had sewn.

Lucas was deep asleep when Lunette floated in on a breeze through the open window. Little Mouse scurried in close behind her. Lunette gobbled the honey cake and saw the note tucked underneath. Little Mouse nibbled the crumbs and then dove beneath Lucas's pillow, looking for the tooth. He crawled out with a small, lumpy ... something.

"It's Lucas's tooth!" Lunette said, and then she read the note aloud.

Dear Small Friend,

I know I must not call you by name.
Maybe I shouldn't even write your name.
And so I will call you the Tooth Fairy.
Thank you for making me less afraid.

Your Friend,
Lucas

P.S. Here's my tooth! Please let me know what you do with it.

Little Mouse left the little star under Lucas's pillow, and they both hurried off.

Back at the hollow, Lunette started to sew.

"We have a lot to do!" she said to her friends. "We must hang this star before sunrise, to surprise Lucas. Flynn, will you add Lucas's tooth to your recipe for magic dust? And, Blossom, please paint the big star with honey, so the dust will stick when we sprinkle it on!"

Once the star was covered with honey, Lunette, Blossom, and Flynn sprinkled it with golden pollen and magic dust. "We must go now—it is almost sunrise!" Lunette called out, leading the way into the night sky.

Lucas awoke before dawn. Looking under his pillow, he found a small
star-shaped pillow with a shiny coin tucked inside. There was a note for him, too.

Dear Lucas,

Thank you for your tooth! It is a lovely gift.
I am sure you were brave when it fell out.
When you awaken, <u>look up</u>. There is something
bright and beautiful in the sky—just for you.
Your tooth helps it sparkle!

Love, Your friend,
the Tooth Fairy

P.S. When you see your surprise in the sky, make a wish!

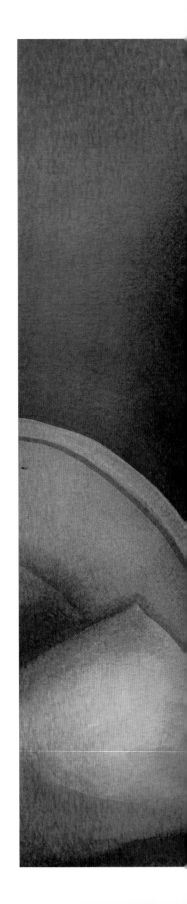

Lucas went to the window and looked up. A star twinkled high above him—the biggest, brightest star in the sky.

"It's *my* star," Lucas said to himself. "Lunette promised to make something magical, and she did!" He closed his eyes and wished for more stars to brighten Moonglow Glen.

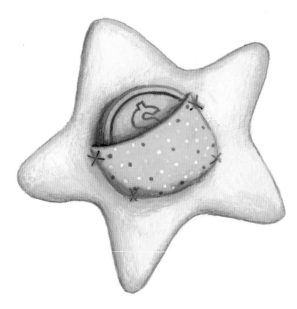

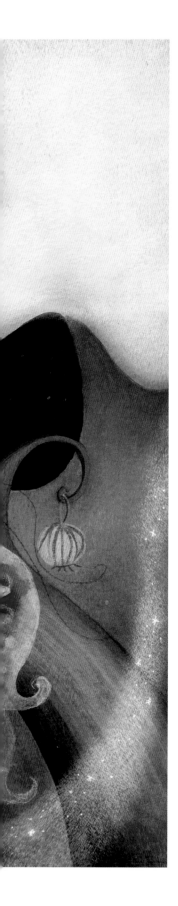

News of the Tooth Fairy spread quickly, throughout the glen and far beyond. Lucas told his friends Liam, Nicole, and Rose. They told Francisco, Liza, and Oliver. And they all told *their* friends about the Tooth Fairy, too.

And so it went ... Lunette and the other fairies were soon making hundreds and then thousands of stars. And to this day, they hang those stars to brighten the night sky, with children's lost teeth sprinkled in as part of the magic.

ONE NIGHT in Moonglow Glen, Lunette and the Fairy Queen looked up at the starry sky. "Lunette," the queen said, "you are brave and clever—just as you hoped to be. But it is your kindness that brightens the glen and the big, beautiful world."

Lunette gazed up at the bright new stars in the sky. She smiled and said, "Good queen, it is more than enough to be brave, clever, and kind. It is truly *special* to brighten the glen and the big, beautiful world, just as I wished. And I am so grateful to be the Tooth Fairy, now and always!"

COMPENDIUM®
live inspired

With special thanks to the entire Compendium family.

CREDITS:
Written by: Robin Cruise
Illustrated by: Valeria Docampo
Designed by: Sarah Forster
Edited by: Amelia Riedler, M.H. Clark & Kristin Eade
Creative Direction by: Julie Flahiff

Library of Congress: 2015941702
ISBN: 978-1-938298-89-9

2nd printing. Printed in China with soy inks. A021604002